*To Mark Klein, one of the strongest, kindest,
and most inspirational friends I've ever known.*
—Frank

*To my best friend, my husband, Barrington, who continues to show me the
meaning of unconditional love and friendship. To my first friend, my sister,
Felicia, who has always believed that I can do anything I put my mind to.*
—Charnaie

For Peter, my best friend forever
—Kayla

Acknowledgments

Without friends, writing a picture book, especially one about friendship, would be
impossible. There are not enough pages for us to acknowledge the many friends who
have helped us along the way—in our lives and in our writing lives. Meeting in person
for the first time, we (Charnaie and Frank) instantly liked each other and we knew we'd
collaborate in the world of children's literature. Having our first venture be this book
about friendship is a blessing. So we are grateful for our families and friends who've
mentored, supported, and inspired us along our journeys. And we are grateful for our
friendship—without it, this book would not have happened.

—Frank and Charnaie

SLEEPING BEAR PRESS™
2395 South Huron Parkway, Suite 200, Ann Arbor, MI 48104
www.sleepingbearpress.com
© Sleeping Bear Press
Printed and bound in the United States.
10 9 8 7 6 5 4 3 2 1

Library of Congress Cataloging-in-Publication Data

Names: Murphy, Frank, 1966- author. | Gordon, Charnaie, author. | Harren, Kayla, illustrator.
Title: A friend like you / by Frank Murphy & Charnaie Gordon ; illustrated by Kayla Harren.
Description: Ann Arbor, Michigan : Sleeping Bear Press, [2021] | Audience: Ages 4-8. |
Summary: "There's nothing in the world like a wonderful friend. Friends are there to laugh with you
and ready with a hug when you need one. Adventure friends and study friends. There are forever
friends and brand new friends. In this book, celebrate ALL the marvelous ways to be a friend!"
— Provided by publisher.
Identifiers: LCCN 2021010661 | ISBN 9781534111127 (hardcover)
Subjects: CYAC: Friendship—Fiction. | Conduct of life—Fiction.
Classification: LCC PZ7.1.M8724 Fr 2021 | DDC [E]—dc23
LC record available at https://lccn.loc.gov/2021010661

A FRIEND like YOU

By Frank Murphy and Charnaie Gordon
Illustrated by Kayla Harren

PUBLISHED BY SLEEPING BEAR PRESS

You'll meet thousands and **thousands** and **thousands** of people in your lifetime.

Some you will only meet once.

Some you'll get to know a little.

And you'll get to know some people so well that you'll call them friends.

Some of these friends will become...
supportive friends,
honest friends,
generous friends.

True friends,

forever friends,

best friends.

Go out into the world and make friends.
The world needs a friend like you!

Be a curious friend.

Asking questions is a good way to start friendships.

Listen with an open heart and mind.

When you are a better listener, you can ask better questions.
Getting to know someone's stories, thoughts, and ideas matters.
It shows you care.

Be an accepting friend.

Some people you meet will be from places that are far, far away.

But most will be from right around the corner.

A few will look
just like you.

A few will practically
be your opposite!

Many will believe what you believe.
Even more will not . . .

Be an open-minded friend.
Become friends with all kinds of people.

The only way to learn how to get along with
people who are different from you is by being with them.
Find out things you both like to do and do them together.

Be a flexible friend.

You might like to wear high-tops, while your friend likes to wear flip-flops.

A friend might like to snack on sushi, but you prefer pizza.

You might stay up all night reading, while a friend spends all night watching movies.

Try something new with a friend!

And no matter what, celebrate each other.

Be a forgiving friend.
Your friends will make mistakes.
You will too.

Everyone makes mistakes.
Friends say sorry and move on . . .

Be a kind friend.

Friends share.

They share things, like toys

and games

and snacks.

But they also
share ideas . . .

. . . and goals and hopes
and dreams.

Sharing makes friendships stronger—
so share often.

Be a thoughtful friend.

When a friend is feeling down,
maybe you'll help them up.

Or maybe their life is feeling loud,
and you can be a quiet place.

Whatever you do, being there when they
need you is what matters most.

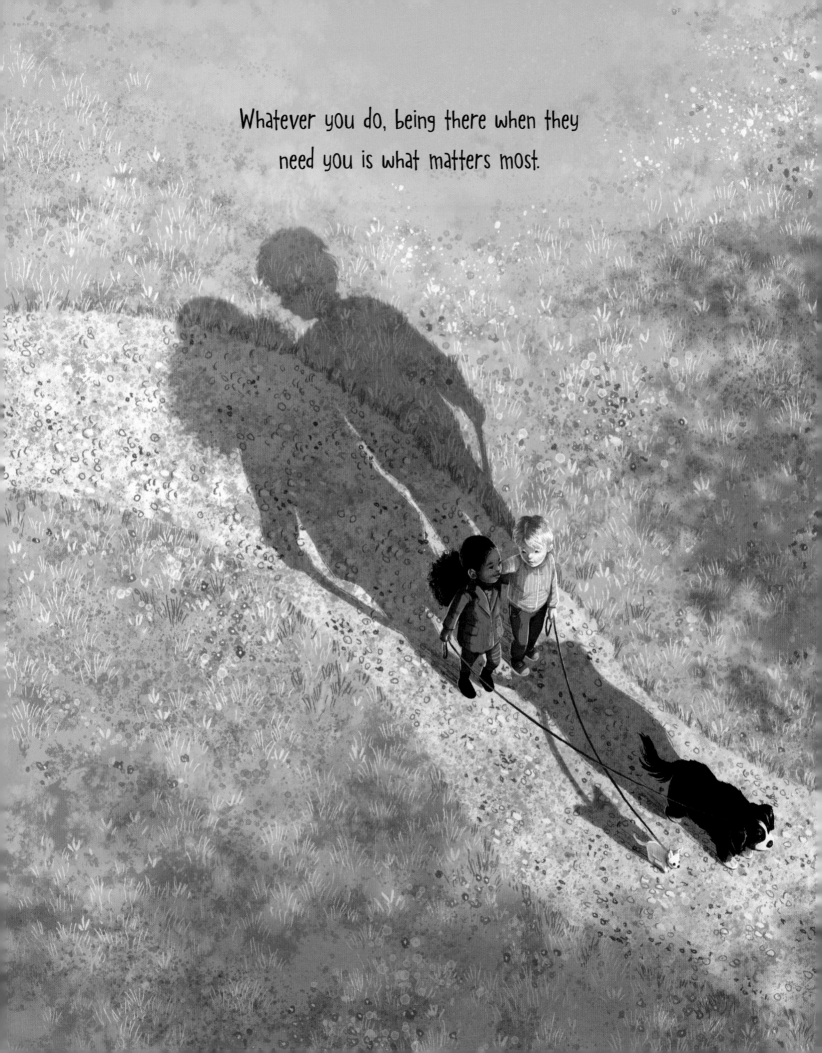

Be an ally.

An ally is one of the most powerful things you can be for a friend.

It means a friend can trust you to stand up and speak up
for them, even when they're not there.

A friend and ally will always have your back.
And you will always have theirs.
That's what true friends do.

It doesn't matter if it's a friend you grow up with
or a friend you meet when you're all grown-up.

Play together.

Laugh with each other.

Dream together.

One day you'll notice—you weren't just having fun,
you were making memories.
The memories you make together will last a lifetime.

So go out into the world and make friends.
Be curious and accepting, forgiving and kind.
Be a true friend.
The world needs a friend like you.

Authors' Note

The bond a person makes with a friend is a little bit like magic. Have you ever heard the phrase *more than the sum of its parts*? Friendships are like that—more than just the combination of two individual people. When people become friends something miraculous happens. They gain compassion and understanding, trust, laughter, and *so much FUN*. And the feeling of friendship is different from any other kind of relationship.

Friendships are among the most precious things we can have; they enrich our lives in so many ways. Good friends teach you about yourself and challenge you to be better. They can also help you understand the importance of allyship, equality, fairness, acceptance, and mutual respect. These things can enable you to use your mind and your voice to influence change.

We hope that this book serves as a celebration of friendships—friendships of every kind. We also hope that it serves as a gentle guide for young people to respect and cherish the friendships they have and will make across the years.

Most importantly, we hope the words and art on these pages inspire people everywhere to see the infinite possibilities we all have with friendships. A friend can be the same and/or different from you in so many ways. Whether it be race, skin color, religion, gender, gender expression, hopes and dreams, age, nationality, abilities, interests, failures, or successes—all of these can be celebrated within friendships. The basic components of any wonderful relationship, from childhood to adulthood, are all founded in friendship.

So get out there and *make a friend*!

Letter Activity

Showing gratitude for the things you have is important. It's especially important to show gratitude for the people you have in your life! Think of a friend who is special to you. Maybe you saw them today at school. Maybe you haven't seen them in a very long time. They might be an old friend, or a brand-new friend. Write them a handwritten letter that lets them know what their friendship means to you. Include a favorite memory and an idea for something to do the next time you see each other. You could also include a drawing or collage.

Ask a teacher or trusted adult to help you mail the letter to your friend!